Up, up and away. . . .

At seven in the morning, the alarm clock beside Andrew's bed started to buzz as usual. As usual, Andrew stretched out a hand to turn it off.

Not as usual, he couldn't reach the clock.

The buzzing continued as his hand flopped about, trying to feel the nightstand beside his bed, trying to find that noisy clock.

He looked down.

Down??

Yes. There was the clock down below him.

In fact, there was his *bed* down below him.

Andrew was floating about three feet above his bed!

MY SECRET IDENTITY ™

starring
Derek McGrath
Jerry O'Connell

Produced by: Paul Saltzman
Line Producer: Brian Walker
Written by: Brian Levant and Fred Fox, Jr.
Directed by: Don McBrearty
Executive Producer: Martin J. Keltz
Co-Executive Producers: Brian Levant, Fred Fox, Jr.
Executive in Charge of Production: Sondra Kelly

Produced by Sunrise Films Limited in association
with Scholastic Productions Canada Ltd.

In association with CTV Television Network Ltd.
with the participation of Telefilm Canada.

MCATV — Exclusive distributor

A Novelization by Jovial Bob Stine
Created by Brian Levant & Fred Fox, Jr.
adapted from the *My Secret Identity*™ pilot episode
written by Brian Levant and Fred Fox, Jr.

AN
APPLE
PAPERBACK

SCHOLASTIC INC.
New York Toronto London Auckland Sydney

ISBN 0-590-42414-9

Cover art by Neal McPheeters.
Cover art designed by Sloan • Millman Productions, Ltd.

12 11 10 9 8 7 6 5 4 3 2   9/8 0 1 2 3 4/9

Printed in the U.S.A.   28

First Scholastic printing, March 1989

1

"A ndrew, why are you eating cookies now? You just had lunch." Mrs. Clements strode quickly across the kitchen and took the oatmeal cookie from Andrew's hand.

"But I'm a growing boy. I'm still hungry," Andrew protested.

"You'd better watch it," his mother said. "You're looking a little pudgy." She raised the cookie to her mouth and took a large bite out of it.

Andrew made a face. "That's what you always say when you want the cookie I'm eating. I'm not pudgy. What you see here is solid muscle." He pulled up the sleeve of his red T-shirt and flexed his arm to make a muscle.

But she had turned away to see what all the noise was in the other room. It was Andrew's little sister, Erin, fighting with one of her friends again.

"Stop it," she called to them. "You've got to stop all this silly fighting."

"But we like to fight," Erin called back. She always had an answer for everything.

Mrs. Clements walked back into the kitchen, sighing wearily. She finished off Andrew's oatmeal cookie, chewing quickly, and turned to him. "Why are you still in here?" she asked.

"I'm waiting for you to leave so I can take another cookie," he said.

They both laughed. Andrew thought his mom looked really pretty when she laughed. Her wavy blonde hair shimmered in the sunlight from the kitchen window. Her blue eyes seemed to light up.

She looked so much younger when she laughed. But she seldom laughed these days. Ever since Andrew's dad had died, she carried a certain sadness with her. It always made him feel good to say something funny that they could laugh at together.

"Pudgy, pudgy," she repeated, pointing at him.

"I am not," he said. "This T-shirt is a little small, okay? I'm fourteen. I'm growing fast."

He reached for the bag of cookies. "At my age, you need a lot of energy."

"It doesn't take much energy to sit around in your room all day reading comic books," she said, the smile disappearing from her face.

"Yes, it does," he said. Then he realized he hadn't meant that. "I mean — I don't just read them, Mom. I'm a collector."

"Yes, yes. Anyone who has piles of comic books under his bed is a collector."

"It's a serious business, Mom. I could make serious money." He took a bite of the cookie before she changed her mind. One cookie wasn't going to be enough, he realized. He was going to need at least two, or maybe three.

"Speaking of money, Andrew — "

He didn't like any sentence that started with "speaking of money."

"Don and Ron are coming over any minute," he said, quickly interrupting. "I think they're interested in buying one of my comics. It could mean really big money."

"Speaking of money, Andrew," his mother repeated, "aren't you supposed to mow Dr. Jeffcoate's lawn this afternoon?"

"Oh. Right." He had completely forgotten. "I didn't forget," he said. "I'll get over there right after I make the deal with Don and Ron."

They heard a loud crash outside. "Hmmmmphhh gmmmmph?" Andrew asked, his mouth full of oatmeal cookie.

"Just those movers," his mother said, shaking her head. "Someone's moving into the Walters house across the street. But the movers can't seem to get any furniture out of the van without dropping it at least once." She turned to look toward the living room door.

Using all of the speed and stealth at his command, Andrew pulled two more cookies from the bag.

"I see what you're doing!" she cried.

She really did have eyes in the back of her head.

"Uh . . . they're not for me. They're for Ron and Don," he told her. Little white lies didn't count. Little white lies about cookies didn't count at all!

There was another crash, this time from the den. She hurried to see what Erin and her friend were up to.

Andrew took the cookies and headed to his room. On the way, he stopped in front of the full-length mirror in the hallway.

"Pudgy? What does she mean pudgy?" he asked, examining himself carefully in the mirror.

So, he had a slightly round face. All of the Clem-

4

entses had round faces. It was a family tradition. That didn't mean he was pudgy.

He studied himself seriously. He wasn't that bad-looking, he decided. Nice, brown hair, just wavy enough. He probably should let it grow a little longer. Blue eyes that were friendly — and intelligent. A few freckles on his nose, just to drive the girls wild.

"Not a bad-lookin' dude," he said aloud, giving himself a thumbs-up. "What did she mean pudgy?"

He took a big bite from one of the cookies in his hand. The doorbell rang. He swallowed quickly. "I'll get it!" he yelled.

2

Erin was already at the door when he got there. "Andrew isn't home," she was telling them.

She was only eight, but she had a sense of humor that could cause a lot of trouble when she wanted to — which was always.

"Don't listen to her, guys. I'm here," Andrew said, pushing her gently away from the screen door.

"Prove it," she said, pushing him back. Eight-year-olds could be a real pain. She was kind of cute, though, with her red hair and the big, round, yellow-framed glasses she always wore, and the baseball cap that she pulled down over her head.

"Don and Ron — that rhymes!" she told Don and Ron.

"What rhymes with get lost?" Andrew asked. He pushed open the door so Don and Ron could

6

come in. "We've got serious business, right, guys?"

"How's it goin', Andrew?" Don said, grinning as usual. He never stopped grinning, no matter what was going on. It was as if his face were just frozen like that. Some kids thought he was goofy. But he was Andrew's friend, so Andrew tried not to think about it.

Ron, on the other hand, looked serious. He had dark brown, serious eyes, and he always seemed to be thinking serious thoughts. But he was just as goofy as Don, Andrew thought.

They were the perfect guys to sell comic books to. They were new collectors, so they didn't know as much about it as Andrew. And they were kind of gullible, so they'd pretty much believe whatever he told them.

And Andrew knew just about everything there was to know about comic books. He had comic books, carefully wrapped in clear plastic comic book bags, tacked up on his bedroom wall. And he had cartons of comics, carefully indexed by title and company.

He loved comics. He loved everything about them — the bright colors, the cheap paper, the smell of the ink, the cluttered ads, the tiny type on the Letters pages.

7

And most of all he loved the superheroes. Andrew was a walking encyclopedia when it came to superheroes.

He could tell you that Ant-Man first appeared in *Avengers* #1. Or that the complete origin of Captain America wasn't revealed until *Captain America* #255. Or that Air-Walker made his final appearance in *Thor* #306.

Ron was into mutants. And Don was into surreal creations like ninja turtles and heavily armed hamsters.

But Andrew preferred the good, old-fashioned crime fighters. The Flash. Daredevil. Even Superman if the writers weren't being too silly.

How great it would be, he thought, to walk around in your secret identity like a normal guy, fooling everyone into thinking you were just some nerd. Then when trouble struck, to spring into action, to use your amazing powers, defeat the evil enemy, and fly home with the thanks and admiration of the entire world.

Not a bad life at all.

Don and Ron tossed aside some of Andrew's clothes that cluttered the floor and sat down on the carpet. Andrew pulled a carton of comics out from under his bed and began searching through them.

"A bunch of guys were playing softball behind school this morning," Don said, balling up a pair of Andrew's dirty socks and tossing them from hand to hand. "You know that tenth-grader Mulholland? The one that looks like a gorilla?"

"Yeah, I've seen him," Andrew said. "Did you bring him a banana?"

"You kidding? I wouldn't mess with him. He hit the ball so hard, he dented it."

"He what??" Andrew looked up from the comics.

"He dented the ball. Really. It wouldn't roll anymore. We had to get another one."

"If the Mighty Thor played baseball, he'd shatter the ball into a million pieces," Andrew said.

Don and Ron didn't say anything. They just looked at each other. They were used to Andrew bringing comic book characters into the conversation. It was like the heroes in the comics were as real to him as the guys on the playground.

"Hey — here it is," Andrew cried, pulling a comic out of a carton. "I think you guys will be very interested in this one." He held it up so they could see the cover.

"What is it?" Ron asked.

"*Journey into Mystery* #83," Andrew told him.

Ron tossed the balled-up socks to Don, who

tossed them back at him. "What's so special about it?" Ron asked skeptically.

Andrew sighed impatiently. "Guys, maybe you didn't hear me correctly. We're talking *Journey into Mystery* #83 — the first appearance of Thor! This is the most important comic of the Silver Age. I'd sooner sell you my dog, but . . . if the offer is right, maybe. . . ."

"It's really valuable?" Don asked, grinning as always.

Andrew could see that he was really interested. But before he could continue his sales pitch, the door of his room swung open and Erin came bouncing in.

"Andrew — "

"Not now, Erin. I'm busy, okay?"

"Mom says you've got to stop what you're doing and go mow Dr. Jeffcoate's lawn."

"Erin, can't you see I'm in top secret negotiations? Out!"

Erin shrugged. "Mom said," she muttered. She turned to leave. Then she saw the comic in Andrew's hand. "That comic's missing a page, you know," she told Ron and Don. She ran out of the room with a mischievous smile on her face.

"We're not interested," Ron said quickly.

Andrew pretended to be shocked. He wasn't

about to give up so easily. "What?" he cried. "You wouldn't go out with a beautiful girl just because she had a spot on her dress?"

Before Don and Ron could get the point of this question, the door swung open again and Erin popped her head back into the room. "Andrew, Mom says if you want to go out with your stupid friends tonight, you'd better get over to Dr. Jeffcoate's."

She closed the door a split second before Andrew's football smacked against it.

"Now, as I was saying — " Andrew started.

"We'll give you twenty-five dollars and *Daredevil* #2 for it," Don said.

"Shut up, Don," Ron said.

"No way," Don told Ron. "If I listened to you, we'd still be collecting stamps!"

"Okay, guys. I believe there is an offer on the floor." Andrew said, trying hard not to reveal how excited and pleased he was.

They were interrupted again by a knock on the door.

"How many times do I have to tell you to leave me alone?" Andrew screamed.

The door opened and Andrew's mother came in.

"Oops. Sorry, Mom," Andrew said. Ron and Don laughed.

11

"Andrew, you've got a job to do," Mrs. Clements said. "Sorry, boys, but you'll have to go home now."

Ron and Don jumped to their feet and headed to the door. "I'll be in touch, guys," Andrew called after them.

"How were the oatmeal cookies?" Mrs. Clements asked.

Ron and Don gave her confused looks. "What oatmeal cookies?"

They disappeared down the stairs.

"Aw, Mom," Andrew wailed, "I was *this* close to unloading a comic for three times what I paid for it!"

"Big business deals will have to wait," she told him, looking around despairingly at the cluttered room. "You've got some real money to earn right now at Dr. Jeffcoate's. You can't spend all your time in a comic book dreamworld."

"I know, Mom," Andrew said quietly. He shoved the comic book carton back under the bed. "I'll do better. I promise."

"Don't make promises, " she said. "Just let me see some results."

"Okay," he said. "I promise." He thought maybe that would make her laugh, but it didn't.

He followed her out the bedroom door and

headed downstairs. He pushed open the screen door and headed slowly down the block toward Dr. Jeffcoate's house.

"Another boring afternoon of mowing Dr. J.'s lawn," he told himself.

Andrew didn't realize that he was minutes away from changing his life forever.

3

Back and forth, back and forth. What was the point of mowing the grass, anyway? It would only grow back in a few days.

Maybe one of these days I'll mow it in circles, Andrew thought. Or maybe in trapezoids. Or parallelograms. That would make the job more interesting.

Dr. Jeffcoate would like that kind of thinking. He was always looking for new ways of doing things, always dreaming up clever new inventions.

Groaning as he pushed the mower, Andrew looked toward the scientist's house. It was a sprawling red brick house with a circular tower in the middle that looked a little like a castle turret. Behind the sliding glass doors in back of the large house was Dr. Jeffcoate's laboratory.

Andrew didn't know for sure what went on in Dr. J.'s lab. But he had a pretty good idea. He had read at least several hundred comic books that featured mad scientists in laboratories that looked just like this one.

Was Dr. Jeffcoate a mad scientist? No. Probably not. He was too nice to be a mad scientist. But Andrew liked to imagine that he was.

The sun beat down as if it were right on top of him, as if it were aiming its rays directly at him. Andrew stopped pushing the heavy hand mower and mopped his wet forehead with his arm. His hands still tingled from pushing the mower. His back ached.

Suddenly he forgot all about how miserable he was. The air became sweet, scented by the fragrance of spring blossoms. The sun became warming instead of oppressive.

What changed Andrew's attitude? Looking across the street, he saw a girl about his age. She was telling the moving men where to put a piece of furniture they had just dropped out of the truck.

"She must be my new neighbor," Andrew told himself. Even from across the street, he could see that she was very pretty, with soft, wavy brown hair, dark eyes, and a beautiful smile.

He stood staring at her for a while — until he realized that she was staring back at him! Then he quickly looked away.

He looked back. She was still there. She *wasn't* a mirage caused by his being out in the sun too long!

She smiled at him. He looked away, embarrassed.

She looked away. He stared at her. She looked back. He looked away.

He mopped his brow again, then pulled off his T-shirt. He flexed his arm hard so she could see how muscular he was. He looked up to make sure she was admiring him.

He was just in time to see the screen door slam behind her. She had gone back into her new house.

Andrew tossed his T-shirt across the lawn and stood staring at the spot on the sidewalk where she had stood. "I wonder what her name is," he asked himself, leaning against the lawn mower handle.

Lost in thought, he didn't hear the garage door open. And he didn't see Dr. Jeffcoate come marching across the yard.

"Andrew — are you mowing my lawn or waiting for a chest X ray?" the scientist demanded.

Andrew quickly snapped out of his reverie. "Oh, hi, Dr. J."

"The name is Jeffcoate."

Andrew shook his head as if he were shaking the picture of the girl out of his mind. He focused on his employer.

In his lab coat, Dr. Jeffcoate looked a lot like a big, white owl. His nose was rather beaklike, and he wore round, owl-like glasses. His face was round and pudgy, as was the rest of him. He constantly walked around as if his feathers were ruffled. He was always worked up about one thing or another.

He always gave Andrew a hard time, and he certainly didn't pay well at all. But Andrew liked him anyway. Dr. Jeffcoate was interesting, Andrew thought, like a comic book character. You could never guess what he was going to say or do next. And he had a twinkle in his eye, a devilish grin that showed he didn't take the world too seriously. Behind his sarcasm, behind his gruff manners, Andrew could tell the scientist really cared about people.

His lab coat flapping behind him, Dr. Jeffcoate pulled a portable gas barbecue from the garage.

"Having a barbecue?" Andrew asked, still leaning on the mower handle.

"You might say that," the scientist said mysteriously. He pulled the barbecue grill around to the side of the house.

Andrew decided to follow him. He had to run to catch up. Dr. Jeffcoate seemed to be in a big hurry.

"You know, Dr. Jeffcoate," Andrew said, walking fast to keep up, "in the few months I've been mowing your lawn, I've come to regard us as more than an employer and employee. I think of us as friends."

"My heart's aglow," Dr. Jeffcoate said, chuckling, "but you're not getting a raise."

Andrew couldn't help but look disappointed.

"Get the hose, will you?" Dr. Jeffcoate demanded, tugging the barbecue grill up to the edge of his property. From the look on the scientist's face, Andrew guessed he had something very serious on his mind.

He ran to get the garden hose, which was hanging on the side of the garage. He carried it to Dr. Jeffcoate, who had set up the grill beneath the drooping boughs of a huge fruit tree that hung over into his yard from next door.

As he walked, Andrew heard a loud, unpleasant *squish*. "What was that?" he cried, stopping.

"Rotten fruit," Dr. Jeffcoate scowled. "This tree

only bears rotten fruit. And it's all over my backyard."

Andrew examined the bottom of his sneaker. Dr. Jeffcoate turned and, raising his hands to his mouth, called up to the balcony of the house next door. "Oh, Mrs. Shellenbach? May I see you for a moment, please?" His voice was light and pleasant.

Dr. Jeffcoate smiled in anticipation, his eyes on the neighbor's balcony. Mrs. Shellenbach's house was even more ramshackle and cluttered than Dr. Jeffcoate's, Andrew noticed.

Suddenly Dr. Jeffcoate removed a pair of safety goggles from his lab coat pocket and handed them to Andrew. "Better put these on," he whispered out of the side of his mouth.

"Why?"

"You'll see."

Mrs. Shellenbach, a large woman with tangles of red hair, wearing a flower print housecoat, appeared on the balcony. She was carrying a small, yapping dog. She and the dog had matching pink bows on their heads.

"What do *you* want?" Mrs. Shellenbach asked, making a face of utter disgust the moment she realized it was Dr. Jeffcoate calling her.

Dr. J. returned her look of disgust with a forced

smile. "Mrs. Shellenbach," he called up to her, "since that sad occasion when I became your neighbor, I have asked that you remove this unsightly tree and its useless, tasteless fruit from my property."

She and the dog in her hands both glared down at him. "Look, cheese brain," Mrs. Shellenbach barked, "I love that tree. So get outta my face." She spun around and started to walk back into her house.

Dr. Jeffcoate kept the smile on his face and pleasant tone in his voice. "Thank you. Sorry to take up your time," he said.

He took several steps back from the barbecue grill, pulling Andrew with him. Then he pulled something out of his lab coat. It was a small black box with an antenna. It looked like a remote control for a TV.

He pulled out the antenna and pointed it at the gas barbecue grill. Then he pushed the button.

With a loud burst, red and yellow flames shot up from the barbecue. The overhanging branches were swallowed up by the flames.

Dr. J. stared intently as the gas fire quickly removed the branches from his property. Then he turned to Andrew with a grin on his face. He was very pleased with himself.

As he turned the garden hose on the smoldering remains, Andrew smiled, too. "That's what I like about Dr. J.," he told himself. "Just when you think he's a crotchety stuffed shirt, he goes and does the nuttiest thing you can imagine!"

"Now, about my raise," Andrew started, returning to his favorite subject.

But Dr. Jeffcoate had already returned to his lab.

4

Half an hour later, Andrew was still pushing the lawn mower across Dr. Jeffcoate's wide front yard. The mower had definitely become heavier. The sun had become even hotter.

"If Dr. J. can invent an instant tree remover, why can't he invent a grass remover?" Andrew asked himself. He realized he had just given himself an idea. He could take the gas barbecue grill and turn it on its side. One blast and the grass would be gone for good!

But then, so would his lawn-mowing job.

Andrew looked across the street. There was the girl again. She was carrying empty cartons to the curb.

Was she smiling at him?

He couldn't tell. The sun was in his eyes.

He smiled back at her, just in case she was smiling at him.

Someone appeared behind her in the driveway. Probably the girl's father. He was fairly young-looking, had dark hair, and was wearing slacks and a gray pullover sports shirt. "Hey, kid," he called to Andrew. "How much do you want to mow my lawn?"

"Oh, more than anything!" Andrew cried.

He was staring at the girl. He didn't realize he hadn't exactly answered the question correctly.

"I'll give you five bucks," the girl's father offered.

"Deal!" Andrew cried eagerly, without really hearing the number.

He smiled at the girl. She sure was pretty!

She looked away shyly.

What a day! Andrew suddenly felt as powerful as those bursting flames from the barbecue. Without realizing it, he was running with the lawn mower, pushing it across the lawn at near supersonic speeds!

There were a million questions he wanted to ask her. Like: What was her name? And: What did she think of him? And: What did she notice about him first that she thought was really terrific?

He knew what was terrific about her — everything!

Soon, he knew, they would be very good friends. More than friends.

She was already smiling at him, after all.

Unless that was just the sun in his eyes.

Andrew was thinking about the girl so intently, he didn't realize the lawn was mowed. He kept pushing the mower over the already cut grass.

Finally, he saw that he was finished. He pulled the mower over to the side of the garage. Wiping his sweaty hands on his T-shirt, he walked over to the side door of Dr. Jeffcoate's house.

He felt tired and over-heated. He knew his face must be bright red. What a workout! He hoped Erin and Robbie had left a few cookies in the bag. He was starving.

He knocked on the side door.

No answer.

He knocked again, a little harder.

Still no answer.

He pulled open the screen door and stuck his head into the house. "Dr. Jeffcoate?" he called. "Dr. Jeffcoate? I need my money now."

The house was cool and dark. And silent. He stepped inside.

"Dr. Jeffcoate?"

No reply.

He stepped reluctantly through the silent kitchen. The living room was at the end of a short hallway. "Dr. Jeffcoate? Are you here?"

No reply.

The living room was filled with books. Books lined the walls in shelves that reached to the ceiling. There were books on the coffee table and books piled on the couch. "I wonder if he's read all of these," Andrew asked himself.

He found his way down another hallway. He peered through an open doorway down some steps. From down below, he heard a low, steady hum.

"These steps must lead to Dr. J.'s lab," he told himself. He started to hurry down the steep stairs. The hum became louder.

"Dr. Jeffcoate? It's me — Andrew. I need my — YAAAIIII!"

He stumbled on the unfamiliar steps and fell forward into the lab — directly into the path of a bright blue electrical ray.

ZZZZZZZZZZZZZAAAAAP!

The blinding blue current swept over him, around him, through him.

He struggled to move away from it. But it held him firmly, crackling and sparkling over his entire body.

It lifted him up, up off the floor, halfway across the large lab.

He couldn't move. He couldn't breathe. He couldn't see.

Everything was blue, shimmering, electric blue. He was floating in the blue ray, breathing the blue ray, living inside the blue ray.

He *was* the blue ray.

This all took an instant. A split second.

An instant later, it dropped him.

He fell hard to the floor.

And everything went from blue to white.

5

First he began to see lights. Then colors. The world was slowly returning.

Everything was a blur at first, a spinning blur. Then the colors stopped spinning. They began to form shapes.

A pink shape emerged above him, a round pink shape. A round pink shape wearing glasses and a very concerned look.

Dr. Jeffcoate was leaning over him, peering eagerly into his eyes.

Andrew realized he was lying on the hard floor. He stared up at the worried scientist.

"Andrew, how do you feel?" Dr. J. sounded very tense.

It took Andrew a little while to form the words. "Okay, I guess."

Dr. Jeffcoate shined a high-intensity light into Andrew's eyes, first one eye, then the other. He

27

held Andrew's eyelids open wide so he could make a thorough check.

"What happened?" Andrew asked.

The back of his head ached. His stomach felt funny. His hands and feet felt all tingly. He felt as if he had banged his funny bone, and the feeling had spread through his entire body.

"Andrew, I'd like you to count backwards from one hundred," Dr. Jeffcoate said softly, still staring into Andrew's eyes. He looked very worried.

"One hundred," Andrew began. "Ninety-nine." He stopped. "Look — I'm fine, Dr. J.," he said impatiently. He suddenly remembered he had another lawn to mow — the new girl's lawn.

He started to sit up, but Dr. Jeffcoate gently held him down.

"I'm fine," Andrew repeated. "I just slipped or something. I've got to get to another job. So if I could just get paid — "

"Paid?" Dr. Jeffcoate cried. He seemed terribly relieved. "Oh, of course, my boy."

The color came back into Dr. Jeffcoate's face. He helped Andrew to his feet. Then he reached into his lab coat and started to pull out bills.

"You know," he told Andrew, smiling and starting to sound more cheerful, "I've been thinking the lawn has been looking extra nice lately. You deserve that raise."

Andrew stared at him in shock. "I do?"

"Yes, you do. You definitely do," Dr. Jeffcoate repeated. "Here's seven. No. Make it ten dollars!"

"Ten dollars??"

"Yes. Here. Take it." He tucked the money into Andrew's hand. Then his concerned look returned and he stared once again into Andrew's eyes. "You sure you feel okay?"

"Yeah. Thanks," Andrew said, shaking Dr. Jeffcoate's hand vigorously. "I don't care what anyone else says. You're a great guy, Dr. J. I mean, Dr. Jeffcoate."

"Dr. J. is fine with me," the scientist declared happily. He put a hand on Andrew's shoulder and led him slowly to the door.

"Okay, Dr. J.," Andrew said, laughing.

"Now you run along," Dr. Jeffcoate said, opening the door for Andrew. "And let me know if you experience any nausea, dizziness, or seizures."

"Okay. And thanks again for the raise!" Andrew declared, heading across the lawn.

He hadn't really heard the last part. He was thinking about the new girl across the street and how he would now have plenty of money to take her out on a date. Or two dates. Or several dates!

* * *

The rest of the day passed quickly. The sun was starting to lower itself behind the trees. The movers had gone. The block was silent except for the chirping of robins and sparrows and the steady whirr of Andrew's lawn mower.

Andrew realized he wasn't tired anymore. In fact, he was feeling very energetic. Maybe it was because it was *her* lawn he was now cutting.

Suddenly, the girl appeared on the front stoop. Andrew stopped mowing. He smiled at her.

She was wearing faded jeans and an oversized man's dress shirt. She looked terrific.

She looked especially terrific because she was carrying a pitcher of cold lemonade and a glass of ice.

"Hi," she called, as she walked quickly up to him. "I thought you might be thirsty."

"Thank you," Andrew said gratefully. "That's very nice of you." Might as well impress her with my suave, good manners, he thought.

"Well, the movers didn't want any, and I'd hate to throw it away," she said.

So she hadn't made it specially for him.

Or had she? And she was too embarrassed to admit it?

That must be it, Andrew thought.

Andrew took the glass and chugged the lemonade down in a single gulp. When he looked up, she was already heading back to the house.

I can't let her get away so quickly. I haven't even learned her name, he thought. "Can I have some more?" he called.

She smiled, a beautiful smile, turned, and came back to pour him another glass.

"So, where you from?" he asked.

"Out west," she told him. "You go to Briarwood High?" she asked, quickly changing the subject.

"Yeah. I'm presently serving a four-year sentence there," he cracked.

She chuckled appreciatively at his joke. "I start there on Monday," she told him.

"Oh. Maybe we have some classes together," he suggested. "What are you taking?"

Her eyes went up as she tried to remember. She had the most beautiful gray-green eyes he'd ever seen.

"Biology, Chemistry, Computer Science, English, and Chinese," she told him.

"Oh, I see. You're coasting this term," he joked.

"Very funny."

He took a deep breath. It was time to make his move. "You know, at our school we have this sacred custom," he started, grinning mischie-

31

vously at her. "The male and female natives pair off with one another, and they go eat or go to a movie — "

"Look — " she interrupted, frowning. She stared beyond him. Her whole face changed, seemed to harden. "I just can't go out with you." She said each word slowly and distinctly.

"I know," Andrew said quickly. He put on his best apologetic face. "I'm being way too pushy. Please. Forget I said anything. Let's just start from scratch."

He held up the lemonade glass as if greeting her for the first time. "Hi. I'm Andrew. What's your name?"

"CAROLINE!"

It was a man's voice.

Andrew looked to the front stoop to see her father standing at the front door. He looked very angry.

"Caroline — get in here right now," he called sharply.

It was her turn to look apologetic. "I've got to go," she whispered. She ran to the house.

"See you at school, Caroline," Andrew called after her.

He smiled up at Caroline's father. But his smile was returned with an icy, angry glare.

6

The next morning at seven, the alarm clock beside Andrew's bed started to buzz as usual. At first, the buzzing became part of Andrew's dream, a confused dream about trying to ride a speeding motorcycle that was twirling out of control.

Gradually, Andrew realized he wasn't dreaming the loud buzzing sound. And soon after he realized that, his brain clicked in to the fact that it was his alarm clock, waking him up on another school morning.

As usual, he stretched out a hand to turn off the alarm.

Not as usual, he couldn't reach the clock.

The buzzing continued as his hand flopped about, trying to feel the nightstand beside his bed, trying to find that noisy clock.

He looked down.

33

Down??

Yes. There was the clock down below him.

In fact, there was his *bed* down below him.

Andrew appeared to be floating about three feet above his bed.

"So it *is* just part of my dream," he told himself.

How to wake up? Should he pinch himself? He tried it. He looked down.

He was still floating in the air.

He tried shaking himself awake.

He seemed to float a little higher.

Funny. He'd never had this much trouble waking up before.

Maybe I *am* awake. The thought struck him suddenly.

Yes. I'm awake. I'm awake and I'm floating above my bed.

Maybe the law of gravity has been repealed, he thought.

"Hey — no time for jokes, Clements," he scolded himself.

Kitty, his dog, was staring up at him, whimpering in disbelief.

Andrew grabbed for the wall. Missed. He tried waving his arms like wings.

He started to float higher.

He kept struggling until he collided with the

ceiling. Then he started slowly to descend.

He made a desperate grab for his sheet, caught it in one hand, then started to float up again, pulling the sheet up with him.

"If only I could control it," he told himself. Kitty stared up at him warily. She looked terribly confused.

Suddenly, Andrew heard Erin's voice from out in the hall. "Andrew — Mom says you'd better get down here right now!"

"I — I'll be down as soon as I can!" he called to his little sister.

He tried kicking his legs, as if he were back floating in a swimming pool. But that didn't bring him any lower.

He heard Erin out in the hall complaining to their mother. "Mom, Andrew yelled at me again."

"I'll see about that," he heard his mother say sharply.

Seconds later, Mrs. Clements burst into the room. She found Andrew standing on the floor holding a pair of heavy dumbbells. As soon as she entered, he started to do exercises with them.

"Andrew, what are you doing?" she asked, shaking her head.

"Working out," he said, holding on to the dumbbells for dear life. If he put them down, he knew he'd go floating back up to the ceiling again.

His mother already thought he was a light-weight. What would she think if she saw him up on the ceiling with the light fixture?!

"Andrew, you know I have a job interview this morning," she said. "You know I need you to help get Erin off to school."

"I'm just not myself this morning, Mom," he told her.

What an understatement!

"I'll take care of everything," he continued. "I promise."

She sighed and reached up to tighten an earring that had come loose. "If I had a dollar for every time you said that, I wouldn't need to find a job."

He continued raising and lowering the dumb-bells.

She turned and walked out of the room.

"Good luck!" he called after her.

Good luck. We're all gonna need good luck, he thought.

He set down the dumbbells. Immediately he drifted up off the floor. "Oh, no," he said aloud. "This can't be happening!"

But it *was* happening.

He floated up fast, like a new helium balloon. His head hit hard against a ceiling beam.

"Ow!" he yelled instinctively. But he realized immediately he had no need to cry out. "Hey, that didn't hurt!" he said in surprise. He rubbed his head where it should have hurt but didn't. "Why didn't that hurt?"

Kitty looked up at him and started barking shrilly. She'd had enough of his foolishness.

Andrew flapped his arms. He felt more like a blimp than a bird. He started to drift down, then suddenly floated back up, banging his head against the ceiling beam again.

Again, it didn't hurt.

"Andrew — are you coming downstairs for breakfast?" his mother called from the front hall.

"Yes. Down!" he managed to reply, flapping his arms desperately.

"Well, breakfast is on the table. I'm already late. Take care of Erin, okay? I've got to go."

"Okay, Mom," he called, hoping she couldn't tell from his voice that he was on the ceiling instead of the floor.

"Hey — Don and Ron are here," his mother called. "Don't get distracted with them and make everyone late for school."

"Don't worry, Mom."

Don and Ron? What were they doing at his house before breakfast, before he even had a chance to figure out how to stay on the ground?

"Think heavy thoughts," he told himself. "Come on — think heavy. Heavy."

He flapped his arms up, up, up. He started to drift down.

"That's it. You're doing it. Think heavy. You're an elephant. You're a hippo. You're the Refrigerator, lining up for the Bears."

Down, down, he went.

His bare feet touched the floor just as Ron and Don walked into his room.

7

"What do you guys want?" Andrew demanded. He didn't want to talk to them. It was taking all of his concentration to stay down on the floor.

He was thinking the heaviest thoughts he could. He was thinking about giant boulders he had seen during a family vacation in Colorado. But still he had the feeling he might fall "up" at any moment.

"We've been thinking about it," Don said, grinning as always, "and we decided we want to do some heavy trading."

Heavy trading?? It will *have* to be heavy this morning, Andrew thought.

Thinking about those massive boulders, he walked carefully toward his bed and started to straighten it.

"What kind of heavy trading?" he asked.

"Hey — why are you walking funny?" Ron interrupted.

"Uh — me?"

"Yeah. You're walking like you're trying to balance or something."

"It's an exercise," Andrew said, thinking quickly. "I do it every morning. I pretend I'm walking a tightrope, see?" He walked a bit, trying to keep his balance, struggling against the urge to let go and float. "It's good for . . . uh . . . the ankles."

Kitty barked twice as if calling him a liar. Only she knew his secret. She'd spill it to them, Andrew thought, if she could.

"We brought you a special comic," Ron said, renewing their negotiations. "We want to make a one-on-one swap."

"For *Journey into Mystery* #83?" Andrew asked, somehow managing to finish making his bed. It was lumpy and crooked, but it was made.

"Yeah," Don said, scratching Kitty's head. The dog growled and edged away. She didn't like Don.

"A one-on-one swap? No cash?"

"Yeah," Don said.

"We've got something good to trade," Ron said, reaching into his backpack and pulling out a comic in a clear plastic bag.

"It better be good," Andrew said. He started to float off the floor but quickly grabbed hold of the bedpost.

"Are you ready for this?" Ron asked, holding the cover away so Andrew couldn't see it. "Are you in a good mood?"

"Yeah, sure," Andrew replied. "I'm in a very up mood this morning. What have you got?"

Ron slowly, tantalizingly turned the cover of the comic book around so that Andrew could see it. "You're not going to believe this, Clements," he said.

"You're right," Andrew said sarcastically. "I *don't* believe it. *Donald Duck*?? You bring me a Donald Duck comic? This is a joke, right?"

Both feet sailed up a few inches off the rug. Think heavy. Keep thinking heavy, he thought, gritting his teeth to make his face heavier.

"It's not just *any* Donald Duck," Ron said, still holding the cover up as if he were doing show-and-tell at school. "It's *Donald Duck #29.*"

He and Don waited for Andrew to react to this news. But Andrew was too busy gritting his teeth and trying to keep his feet on the carpet to react.

"Sorry, guys," he told them, shaking his head.

"But it's not a reprint," Don argued.

"Sorry, guys."

41

"But it's Carl Barks," Ron added. "The whole lead story was drawn by Carl Barks."

"I don't care if it was drawn by Mickey Mouse himself," Andrew snapped. "No deal. No way. I'm just not into Disney."

Ron slowly slid the comic book back into his backpack. He and Don looked terribly disappointed.

"Give me a break, guys," Andrew said. "You know I'm only into superheroes."

"Yeah. I guess . . ." Don said, still grinning despite his disappointment.

"I can't start collecting ducks," Andrew told them. The room was silent for a few moments. Then Andrew added, "But if you happened to come across *Howard the Duck* #1, maybe we could talk."

"Are you kidding?" both Ron and Don cried at once.

"Maybe I could fly to the moon first," Ron declared. "That would be easier."

"Yeah. You can't get *Howard the Duck* #1," Don muttered. "Nowhere. No way."

"Then I guess we don't have anything to talk about," Andrew said.

"Hey, Andrew — these socks are too tight!"

Erin burst into the room. It was time for her daily struggle over socks. "Help me pull them on."

Andrew was holding tight to the bedpost. "Uh . . . not right now, Erin," he said.

"No. Now!"

"Catch you later," Don said. "We'll come back with a better deal for that comic."

"Fine," Andrew said. "I'm not floating anywhere — I mean, *going* anywhere."

Don and Ron headed quickly out of the room.

"Go pick out another pair," Andrew told Erin. "Any pair you want. Then ask your friend Ellen next door to walk you to school, okay?"

Surprisingly, Erin agreed. A few minutes later, Andrew heard the front door slam. He was alone in the house.

He let go of the bedpost. He started to float up, but he quickly thought himself down. "I'm starting to catch on to this," he told himself.

After a little practice, he was able to move across the floor without looking as if he were walking on a tightrope. He walked over to the mirror and picked up a plastic lighter. He flicked it on. Then he held out his hand and moved the flame up to his fingers.

No pain.

And his fingers didn't burn.

He looked at himself in the mirror. "What's happening to me?" he asked aloud.

He still looked like the same Andrew Clements. But. . . .

Something in a corner of the mirror caught his eye. He turned and walked over to the wall where his most valued comics were displayed.

He picked up the *Captain America* comic in the corner. He knew this comic by heart. It contained Captain America's origin story.

He opened it up to the right page. Sure enough, there was Steve Rogers in a science lab, being blasted by radioactive vita-rays and emerging as the mighty Captain America!

The drawing of Captain America being zapped by the rays stirred Andrew's memory. "That's just what happened to me in Dr. Jeffcoate's lab," he realized.

The comics on his wall suddenly seemed to whirl around him. The all-powerful heroes, so magnificent in their capes and costumes, seemed to bound from the covers and surround him. They were all there, the legendary figures he knew so well — Spider-Man, The Avengers, Daredevil, the Hulk. But they seemed different to Andrew now.

Because he realized he was one of them.

And he realized he now knew his destiny in life.

Andrew turned away from his wall of comics. He pulled back his shoulders and strode with new determination into the bright shaft of light pouring down from his skylight.

In true superhero fashion, he looked up into the blazing white light and loudly decreed:

"In brightest day or blackest night, no evil shall escape my sight!"

He thought for a moment, then continued:

"And I vow to fight a never-ending battle against the forces of evil as . . . POWER MAN!"

He stopped, still staring into the light. He closed his eyes, thinking hard.

"No. There already is a Power Man. Erase that."

He thought about it a little while longer.

"Ultra Man?"

Was there an Ultra Man?

Well . . . there had been a Captain Ultra for a short while, starting in *Fantastic Four* #177.

But he had disappeared. And only Andrew would have heard of him, anyway.

Andrew decided to try the name out. He pretended to be a bystander on the street:

"Look — it's Ultra Man!"

"Yeah, that's good," he told himself. "That sounds pretty nifty."

Whew. It was good to have that settled.

He looked back up into the shaft of light and in his deepest voice boldly declared: "Tomorrow the world shall know me as . . . ULTRA MAN!"

There was no lightning bolt. No crash of thunder. No loud background music to herald his new identity.

Andrew decided he'd better hurry to school.

8

A cool breeze rustled the trees as Andrew stepped out into the sun-drenched morning. He closed the front door carefully behind him, straightened the hood on his navy-blue sweatshirt, and headed quickly down the driveway.

When he reached the sidewalk, he stopped to look across the street at Caroline's house. It was late. She had probably left for school long ago. There was no car in the drive. The house was dark. All of the shades and curtains had been drawn.

Strange, he thought. Why cover all the windows on such a pretty day?

Thinking about Caroline, he turned and started jogging toward school. He felt wonderful. A beautiful day. A new girl across the street. New super powers to use whenever he felt like it.

It didn't take much to make him happy.

He was absolutely bursting with the desire to tell someone what had happened to him. But who could he tell? Superheroes weren't supposed to blab about their secret identities to anyone. Otherwise they wouldn't be secret identities anymore. And if everyone knew who you were, then you'd be vulnerable to attack at all times.

Andrew didn't like the sound of that. But just the same, he wished he had someone he could tell.

He was passing by Dr. Jeffcoate's house just as the scientist came out to get his morning newspaper. Even though it was only about eight o'clock, Dr. Jeffcoate was already fully dressed, with his customary bow tie in place, and a clean, white lab coat over his clothes.

He walked up quickly to Andrew, looking concerned. "Andrew, hi," he said, looking him up and down. "You're feeling all right — aren't you?" The scientist couldn't disguise the worried tone in his voice.

"I'm feeling super!" Andrew declared. He was smiling so broadly, his face looked about to pop. He knew he couldn't keep it in, couldn't keep his secret from Dr. Jeffcoate. He had to tell him. He just *had* to!

"You know, Dr. J.," he began, grinning even

wider, "it was no accident I wandered into your lab yesterday."

"Huh?" Dr. Jeffcoate looked confused.

"It was fate," Andrew continued, talking quickly, excitedly. "Whatever that blue light was, it gave me powers and abilities far beyond those of mortal man."

The confusion left Dr. Jeffcoate's face. He began to look worried.

"Yesterday," Andrew continued, "I was Andrew Clements, mild-mannered high school student. But today, thanks to you — "

He placed his hands on his hips, pulled back his shoulders, and thrust his chin out boldly. "Today . . . I am ULTRA MAN!"

Andrew waited for Dr. Jeffcoate to look as pleased and excited as he was. But the look of concern didn't leave the scientist's owlish face.

He stared at Andrew in silence for a long while. Then he put an arm around the boy's shoulders and led him slowly into his lab.

"Sit down in that chair over there," he instructed Andrew softly, guiding him over to a high-backed leather chair against the equipment-cluttered wall.

"But I'm late for school," Andrew protested.

"It can wait," Dr. Jeffcoate said, still talking very softly, the way a doctor would talk around a very sick patient.

He took out his high-intensity light and directed it once again into Andrew's eyes. "Super powers, eh?" he said, leaning down over Andrew to examine his eyes thoroughly.

"Yeah," Andrew replied enthusiastically. "You know. Like Superman. Well, not as good as Superman's. But better than Aquaman's!"

Andrew was talking very loudly and very fast. But who could blame him for being excited?

"In the last half hour," he told the concerned scientist, "I've discovered I can fly — actually fly. Well, it's more like floating, I guess. But it's about the same as flying."

"Really," said Dr. Jeffcoate softly, shaking his head. He sounded very skeptical.

"I've got super speed, too," Andrew continued, the words pouring out of him like water over Niagara Falls. "Unfortunately, no super strength. But I *am* invulnerable. That means nothing can hurt me."

"I *know* what invulnerable means," Dr. Jeffcoate said, sounding surprisingly touchy.

Andrew decided to ignore it. "Isn't this the most

incredible thing?" he gushed. "Who would ever believe that I would be chosen, that I would be given the special powers to use in the battle against evil?"

Dr. Jeffcoate sat down across from Andrew with a loud sigh. "Andrew," he said, putting down his examining tools, "the other day, you said we were friends, remember?"

"Uh . . . sure," Andrew replied.

"Well, you were right. We *are* friends. That's why I'm going to be frank."

"Frank?" He had just told Dr. J. the most astounding news. Why was he being so gloomy about it?

Dr. Jeffcoate pulled off his glasses and rubbed his eyes. "The photon beam you came in contact with," he told Andrew, "is part of an experiment I'm conducting in genetically altering seeds."

"I don't understand," Andrew said.

"I'm trying to take ordinary seeds and turn them into super seeds so that they'll produce more food, healthier food, plants that can withstand any type of weather — "

"Gee," Andrew interrupted. "And all I came up with for my science project was a wind sock!"

"Andrew, listen," Dr. Jeffcoate pleaded. "Your

exposure to that ray has somehow affected your ability to tell the difference between what's real and what isn't real."

Andrew looked back at him, astonished. "You mean you don't believe me?"

Dr. Jeffcoate climbed to his feet and replaced his glasses. He turned his back on Andrew and began pacing the room. "It's not that I don't believe you. It's just that . . . I don't believe you."

"Well, I — "

"I can't believe you!" Dr. Jeffcoate turned back to face Andrew.

But Andrew was gone.

"Hey — where are you?" He spun around, looking for Andrew. After making a full circle, he still couldn't spot him.

"Eh, what's up, Doc?" Andrew called.

Dr. Jeffcoate looked up to the voice. Andrew was casually floating in the air, his legs crossed, his back against the ceiling.

The scientist suddenly turned as pale as his lab coat. He stared up at the boy floating above his head. He opened his mouth to say something, but no sound came out.

"Dr. J., give me a hand," Andrew called, laughing triumphantly. He stuck out his hand. Dr. Jeffcoate reached up and grabbed it, and pulled Andrew back down to the floor.

"See? See?" Andrew cried happily.

Dr. Jeffcoate was busily taking his own pulse.

"Too big of a shock, huh?" Andrew said, laughing. "Let me get you something to drink."

Dr. Jeffcoate started to say something. But Andrew turned on his super speed. He became a blur of light, and had vanished from the room before the startled scientist could make a sound.

Less than two seconds later, Andrew reappeared. He screeched to a stop in front of Dr. Jeffcoate. The soles of his sneakers were smoking!

"Here. Have some orange juice."

Dr. Jeffcoate was nearly too stunned to speak. "How . . . did you do that?" he managed to stammer.

"Well, I looked in the freezer, found a can of orange juice concentrate, opened it, poured it into a pitcher along with some water, stirred it, poured it into a glass, and brought it to you," Andrew said, very pleased with himself and with the way things were going.

"In two seconds?" Dr. J. cried. "How did you move so fast? It was some kind of trick, right?"

"No trick, Dr. J. I told you. I've got super powers."

Andrew suddenly remembered something he'd been working on before leaving the house. "Oh — wait. You've got to take a look at these. The sketches for my uniform. . . . "

He pulled the sketches from his jeans pocket and handed them to the still-startled scientist. Andrew had colored them in quickly with different-colored markers.

Dr. Jeffcoate grabbed the sketches and tossed them aside without looking at them.

"You don't like the colors?" Andrew asked, sounding hurt.

Dr. Jeffcoate put a firm hand on Andrew's shoulder and looked him in the eyes. His normally smooth face was creased with worry.

"Andrew," he said seriously, "these are real concerns — not comic book fantasies. Who knows what those gamma rays are doing to you?"

For the first time, Andrew began to sense that what was happening to him might not be entirely fun and games. "Gamma rays?" he asked uncertainly.

"I'm afraid so," Dr. Jeffcoate said, sitting down and motioning for Andrew to sit down across from him.

"I've been zapped with gamma rays," Andrew repeated, suddenly as serious as the scientist. "And you don't really know what they'll do to me?"

"Not really," Dr. Jeffcoate said. "My experiment was for seeds, not people."

"And I'm a people. Not a seed," Andrew said slowly, thinking hard about this.

They sat in silence for a while, each one lost in his own thoughts.

Dr. Jeffcoate was the first to speak. "Look, Andrew, this is all my fault," he said. "But what happened here may well be reversible. We'll run some tests. We'll find a way to get you back to normal."

"Back to normal?" Andrew asked, sounding doubtful. "Are you sure?"

Dr. Jeffcoate didn't reply.

At that very moment, only a few miles away, a man sat in seat 23-A of a 727 jetliner headed toward Andrew's town. The man's name was Beech, and in his lap he held a very expensive attaché case.

At about the time Andrew was realizing that having super powers might be more dangerous than he had first imagined, Mr. Beech was listening to the stewardess announce that the plane was about to land.

A tight smile spread over Mr. Beech's narrow face. He adjusted the jacket of his expensive, designer business suit. Then he clicked open the attaché case and reached inside for the photographs he had been pondering the entire plane ride.

He pulled the black-and-white photos out and studied them one more time. The first photo was of Caroline, the girl who had moved across the street from Andrew. She looked a little younger in it. It was a blow-up of a school picture taken the year before.

The other photo was of Caroline's father. He looked a little different, too. Especially his hair, which was lighter and worn in a longer style. But it was definitely Caroline's father.

Mr. Beech stared at these photos, burning the images into his mind. Then, as the plane began to descend, he replaced them carefully in the attaché case, and clicked it shut.

A look of calm but grim determination settled over Mr. Beech's face. Soon his face froze into a look as hard as sheet metal. He had a job to do in this town. And before he did a job, he always made sure that he was in the right frame of mind. He always made sure that he was ready.

Andrew, of course, had no way of knowing that Mr. Beech's job would involve him — and a fight for his very life!

9

Out into the dark night Andrew went. The wind blew hard, swirling his sweatshirt hood behind him like a cape.

It felt different walking down the dark, empty street at night, knowing he had powers that other people didn't. He felt taller, more confident, more mature.

The twisting shadows under the streetlights held no fear for him. He walked in darkness unafraid. He wouldn't run from anything.

Why should he?

He was Ultra Man, after all.

He wouldn't run from trouble.

He'd seek trouble out.

Wherever danger lurked, he'd be there. Wherever the forces of evil tried to force their will on the good people of his town, he'd be there to drive them back.

Something moved in the tall hedges to his left. He steeled himself, harnessing his powers, concentrating his energies in case he had to strike — and strike fast.

Was something waiting for him around the corner of the hedge? Was someone intent on testing his powers, testing his courage?

Ultra Man would pass any test.

Whoever it was had chosen the wrong superhero to mess with.

He burst suddenly into super speed and whipped around the corner of the hedge so fast the human eye couldn't detect him.

There was no one there.

Let that be a warning to anyone who might dare to challenge him. He was too fast for them, too fast for anyone.

He spun around quickly, in case they were sneaking up on him from behind. But there was still no one there.

Another victory for Ultra man.

This was fun, he decided. It was fun being someone new. It was fun feeling so different, feeling so powerful, so in control.

He suddenly wondered why the heroes in the comic books never talked about how much fun it was. Sure, the X-Men had a lot of overwhelming challenges, a lot of powerful enemies. But when they were sitting around Professor X's mansion relaxing and shooting the breeze, why didn't Nightcrawler ever turn to Wolverine and say, "Golly, being a superhero is fun, isn't it?"

Because it was fun to know that you could do things that ordinary mortals wouldn't even try.

The squeal of car brakes made him turn back. A large, black car swerved around the corner, its engine roaring as it picked up speed.

Wait! Someone was just starting to cross the street up ahead.

The car didn't slow down. Didn't the driver see her?

It's Caroline, he realized as the car picked up more speed. She was in the middle of the street. She seemed to freeze there, uncertain of whether to run forward or go back.

The speeding car was just a few yards away.

"No problem!" he cried.

His super speed carried him easily ahead of the car. He scooped her into his arms and floated up, up above the street, up above the trees.

The car sped by underneath them.

He floated gently down until her feet touched the ground.

She didn't move. She kept her arms around

his neck and smiled at him in gratitude and disbelief.

"Andrew," she said, "I didn't know you were Ultra Man!" Her eyes filled with admiration as she hugged him tighter.

This *is* fun! he thought.

"Can you give me an example?"

Huh?

"Can you give me an example?" A woman's voice asked. The voice was familiar. Who was she? Where was she?

"Andrew, can you give me an example?"

He blinked and looked up into the amused face of Mrs. Clarke, his third period English teacher.

"Uh . . . what, Mrs. Clarke?"

"Well, I think you have given us all a perfect example of the effects of daydreaming in class," his teacher said. Everyone, he realized, was laughing at him. Mrs. Clarke looked very pleased with herself.

He looked down the row. Caroline was laughing, too.

Didn't she realize he had just saved her life? Sure, it was only in a daydream. But he could save her life if she needed him to.

He shook his head. Maybe that blue ray *had* affected his brain.

61

Why on earth would Caroline need him to save her life?

After class, Don came up and slapped him on the back. "Way to go, Clements," he said, grinning gleefully.

"Give me a break," Andrew said, gathering up his books and looking to see where Caroline was headed.

She was already out the door.

"Mrs. Clarke called on you eight times," Don told him. "But you just sat there staring out the window."

"So?"

"We thought maybe you died or something." He laughed. That was Don's idea of a really good joke.

"So?" Andrew repeated. He was too annoyed with himself to form any whole sentences.

Don shrugged. "I guess you didn't hear her because you were thinking so hard about our comic book deal."

"What comic book deal?" Andrew asked, stuffing his notebook into his backpack. He deliberately avoided looking at Mrs. Clarke as he walked past her desk to get out the door.

"You know," Don said, hurrying to keep up with him. *"Donald Duck* for *Journey into Mystery."*

Andrew sighed. "Get real, Don. I told you this morning — no way."

"I may be able to throw in a *Silver Surfer* illustrated novel," Don said.

"I already have it," Andrew told him, hurrying down the hall. He thought he saw Caroline turning the corner by the gym.

"Later!" Don called after him.

Andrew turned the corner and saw Caroline talking to another girl. He'd planned to ask her if she wanted to walk home with him.

She looked up. She seemed to see him.

He started jogging toward her.

Her face formed a frown. She turned and went the other way, walking very quickly, and disappeared into a crowd of kids.

"Hey," Andrew asked himself, "is she deliberately avoiding me?"

10

Andrew, are you doing your homework?"

"Yeah, Mom!" he shouted down from the upstairs bathroom. Actually, he wasn't doing his homework. He was washing up. But he had every intention of doing his homework sometime that night.

"How about Erin? Is she in bed?"

"I don't know." Erin was strangely silent. That could only mean she was up to no good. She certainly wouldn't have gone right to sleep.

Andrew dried his face with a big bath towel. He smiled at himself in the medicine chest mirror. "Lookin' good," he said aloud.

But what was that smell?

He picked up a can of spray deodorant. "Wouldn't hurt," he told himself.

He pushed the top of the aerosol can. The deodorant came spraying out.

"Whoa!"

The force of the spray was enough to send him flying up off the floor.

"Wow!" he cried. "Cool!"

He pushed the spray can again. It sent him flying up higher, almost to the bathroom ceiling.

Then he aimed the can at the ceiling and sprayed. It sent him quickly back down to the floor. "Okay!" he cried.

He grabbed another can off the shelf. Now he had one in each hand.

He sprayed them both downward, and went sailing up to the ceiling. He aimed both cans at the ceiling, and shot himself back down to the floor.

Then he sprayed them both to one side. He began twirling in the air like a top.

"All right!" he cried.

"Hey — what's that smell?" Erin called from outside the bathroom door. "Hey, Mom — Andrew's spraying himself with smelly stuff!"

Andrew quickly sprayed himself down to the floor and put the two deodorant cans back on the shelf. "Go away, Erin. Mind your own business," he called.

But Erin had already run back to her room.

Andrew was halfway back to his room when his

mother called. "Andrew, may I come up?"

He stopped at the door to his room and looked in. It looked more like a flea market than a bedroom. There were piles of dirty clothes all over the floor and chairs. Books were tossed everywhere — except on the bookshelves. Papers, notes, games, sports equipment of all types, things he didn't even recognize were scattered all over.

"Just a minute, Mom," he called down to her.

He stepped into his room and went into super speed. He became a blur of light, a tornado force wind, sweeping through his room, picking everything up and putting it in its place.

The room was clear and clean — in less than three seconds!

Andrew took a second to admire his work. Then he sat down at his desk and opened a book.

"Okay. Come on up, Mom."

When Mrs. Clements entered the room, she stopped in the doorway in shock. "Andrew — "

He looked up slowly from his book. "Yes?"

"Your room — it's — "

"Yes?"

"It looks very nice," she said, still looking as if she didn't believe what she was seeing. "I'm impressed."

"Oh, it's nothing," Andrew said nonchalantly. "A guy doesn't want to live like a pig, you know." He put the book down and smiled at her.

She walked over to him and handed him a plastic shopping bag. "For you," she said.

It was his turn to look surprised.

"I've been a little tough on you lately," she said, putting a hand on his shoulder. "I guess I've been pretty tense, what with trying to find a job and everything."

"I understand," he told her.

"Well, I wanted to . . . uh. . . . Well, I bought you a new shirt. Take a look at it."

He pulled open the bag. It was a red-and-white striped pullover. "Hey, it's great," he told her, pulling it out of the bag to look at it better.

She smiled. "A boy should look his best when he's trying to make a good impression on someone."

He could feel his face getting red. How did his mother know about Caroline?

He thought about Caroline deliberately avoiding him in school that morning.

"You should have saved your money, Mom," he said glumly.

She gave him a sympathetic look. "Girl problems?"

"I don't know. I just can't figure it out." He folded up the shirt carefully and set it down beside him on the desk. "One day Caroline brings me lemonade, and the next day she acts like I'm the Invisible Man."

His mother leaned down and kissed him quickly on the side of his forehead. "Well, don't give up," she said. "She hasn't seen you in this shirt yet."

He tried to concentrate on his social studies text. But it's hard to think about the Separation of Powers when you'd rather be thinking about super powers.

Or about Caroline.

Maybe she wasn't avoiding him. Maybe she just hadn't seen him that morning.

"It can't be easy for her," he told himself. "A new girl in a big, new high school, coming in mid-term like that. It's no wonder she always seems a little tense, a little frightened."

He slammed the textbook shut. "Maybe I'll go over there right now," he told himself. "You know, just to see how she's doing, see if she needs any help or has any questions about school."

He decided he'd just be casual about it. Just drop by. Nothing special.

But maybe he'd put on the new shirt anyway. It couldn't hurt.

He pulled on the shirt, combed his hair, brushed his teeth again, and checked himself out in the mirror.

Not bad. He looked very casual. Very cool.

He tiptoed silently down the steps. He didn't want his mother to hear him go out. He'd probably be back in a minute or two anyway. It was pretty late. Caroline might have already gone to sleep.

He stepped out the front door into the darkness. A pale half-moon floated in the black sky. The air was cool and smelled fresh. Crickets chirped loudly. A dog howled somewhere down the block.

He suddenly felt like howling, too. But he held it in and trotted across the street.

The front of Caroline's house was dark. It looked as if all the curtains and shades were still drawn. But Andrew saw a light in back. He headed toward the back door, then stopped.

"What am I doing out here?" he asked himself.

"Going to see Caroline," he answered his own question.

"But it's so late."

"It isn't that late. Remember, you're fourteen. You're not a kid."

"But — "

"Stop arguing," he reprimanded himself.

He walked up to the back of the house and, standing on tiptoe, peered into the kitchen window. Caroline was in the kitchen. She was drying a few remaining dinner dishes.

She had her hair pulled back and tied in a pony-tail. She appeared to be singing as she dried the dishes. Andrew thought she really looked pretty.

He knocked on the window.

She didn't hear him.

He knocked again, a little harder.

Her eyes went wide. She almost dropped the plate in her hand. "Andrew?"

She hurried to the screen door. "It *is* you! You scared me." Her voice was a soft whisper. He could barely hear her.

"Can I come in?" he asked.

"Ssshhhh," she said, putting her finger to her lips and looking nervously behind her.

"I've got to talk to you," he said, pressing his hands against the door and leaning in close to her.

"Andrew — what on earth — ?" she whispered. She looked behind her again. She seemed very nervous. "I'm sorry. It's so late." She looked up at the kitchen clock.

He pressed his forehead against the door. "Just

for a minute?" he asked, whispering.

"No. You can't. I mean, I can't." She dried her hands on the dish towel even though they were already dry.

"Look, Caroline," Andrew said through the screen, "I like you a lot, and I think you like me, too. So why won't you go out with me?"

She stared back at him. She didn't say anything.

"Is it your dad?" Andrew asked.

Caroline looked behind her to the kitchen entranceway. Then she turned back to Andrew and pushed open the screen door. He stepped quickly into the kitchen before she changed her mind.

"Andrew, it's not Dad," she whispered, "and it's not you. I just can't see anyone right now."

Andrew suddenly had a heavy feeling in the pit of his stomach. He took her hand. "Caroline — are you dying?"

Her eyes filled with surprise. Then she laughed. She pulled her hand out of his. "No," she told him. "I'm not dying. You've been watching too much TV!"

She laughed again, but he didn't join her. "But why won't you go out with me?" he demanded.

The smile faded from her face, and her eyes grew cold. She suddenly looked very sad.

"Why?" he repeated.

71

"You'd better go now," was all she said.

He turned and started back out the door. He felt as if he had somehow failed. Even in this new striped shirt he had failed.

But, wait, he thought suddenly. I am Ultra Man. I can't fail. I'm not Andrew Clements any longer. He might give up easily and retreat to his room to daydream. But Ultra Man has powers way beyond those of mortal men. Ultra Man cannot be defeated.

Or, at least, Ultra Man could try one more time.

He stepped back into the kitchen. Caroline turned around, surprised.

"Look," he said, "I've got to walk home from school. You've got to walk home from school. What do you say we do it together?"

Caroline looked away. "I — I can't do that," she said softly.

Andrew sighed and hung his head. First he had been defeated. Now Ultra Man had been defeated, too.

"But I *can* meet you at the Burger Barn at five o'clock," Caroline added, smiling at last.

Andrew smiled back. Then he floated all the way home without realizing it.

11

On the practice field behind the stadium, the cheerleaders were in formation. "All right, let's see some energy now!" Miss Bishop, their coach, called from the sidelines. "I want to see height, and I want to see precision."

"So do I!" one of the cheerleaders in the back row yelled.

Everyone broke formation, laughing. The sun was hot. The blue-and-white wool cheerleader sweaters were uncomfortable. It was hard to concentrate.

"Please, please! Save your energy for your cheerleading!" Miss Bishop pleaded. "I know it's hot out here. But use the heat. Use the energy of the sun. Channel it into your own energy source."

As the cheerleaders reluctantly resumed their places, a tall man stepped onto the practice field.

His cropped white hair was swept straight back, revealing a broad, square forehead. His eyes were small and gray and mean.

Despite the heat of the sun, his expensive dark suit was smooth and unwrinkled. His tie was tightly knotted beneath his square chin.

Mr. Beech walked with long, quick strides, his eyes surveying each cheerleader's face as he approached them. He frowned into the sun. He always frowned. It was his only expression.

Things had not been going well for Mr. Beech in this town. The rent-a-car he had hired at the airport had stalled a few miles after he had picked it up.

When he finally got to the motel on the edge of town, they had lost his reservation. "No vacancies," the desk clerk had said, with a shrug and a helpless smile.

But something in Mr. Beech's eyes, something in that cold, evil glare, something in the slight bulge beneath Mr. Beech's well-tailored jacket that could very well be a pistol in a shoulder holster, had made the desk clerk suddenly remember that there was a room available after all.

After that, Mr. Beech had suffered through a tough sirloin and a cold baked potato. Then he spent a nearly sleepless night on a mattress as hard as a two-by-four.

None of this had helped Mr. Beech's mood as he approached the high school practice field. Which suited him just fine.

Because Mr. Beech *liked* to be in a bad mood.

In fact, when he was doing a job, he *had* to be in a bad mood.

He watched the cheerleaders doing their routine, the frown becoming a sneer of disapproval. "These kids are pitiful," he told himself.

"Very good! Very good! Now one more time!" Miss Bishop was calling to them.

Mr. Beech walked up to her before she could start them up again.

She looked up at him, and uttered a small, involuntary cry of fear and surprise. He liked it when people were immediately afraid of him. He did have a startling appearance. He was nearly seven feet tall. His stark white hair and steel-gray eyes never failed to impress.

"Can I help you?" Miss Bishop stammered, taking a step back.

Mr. Beech stepped even closer to her. He knew it really made people uncomfortable if you stood too close to them.

"I'm Detective Beech," he lied. He pulled a phony silver badge from his jacket pocket and flashed it quickly in front of her face. "I wonder if you can help me with a police investigation."

"Uh . . . sure," Miss Beech said, going pale.

Mr. Beech reached again into his jacket pocket and pulled out a photograph. It was a photo of Caroline, the same one he had been studying on the plane.

"I'm trying to locate this girl," he said, shoving the photo under Miss Bishop's nose. "Ever see her?"

"Yes," Miss Bishop answered quickly. "I've seen her around. She goes to this school."

Mr. Beech replaced the photo in his jacket pocket. He closed his eyes and allowed a tight, satisfied smile to spread across his face.

This job was going to be a breeze. . . .

12

"Now we're just going to take a little blood," Dr. Jeffcoate said, preparing his hypodermic needle.

It was dark and cool in the lab. Andrew had felt relaxed, sitting in Dr. Jeffcoate's big, leather chair, looking at the flickering video screens and other fascinating lab equipment. He had felt relaxed until the scientist had made that announcement.

Now he wasn't so sure. "I really don't like needles too much," Andrew said.

Dr. Jeffcoate smiled down at him. "How unusual," he said. "Just sit back and close your eyes. This will only pinch for a second."

But when he attempted to insert the needle in Andrew's arm, the needle wouldn't puncture the skin.

"Hmmm. Tough skin," the surprised scientist muttered.

Dr. Jeffcoate pushed again, a little harder. It still didn't work. On his third attempt, the needle bent and broke off!

Andrew laughed. "Wow!" he exclaimed excitedly. "The same thing happened in the first issue of *Superman!*"

Dr. Jeffcoate stared at his broken hypodermic needle. Then he gave Andrew a disapproving look. "Andrew," he said, "if I were you, I'd spend a lot less time reading comics, and start cracking my school books so I could get somewhere in life."

"You know, that's really good advice," Andrew said, getting to his feet and walking around the cluttered lab. "I don't know why everyone in the neighborhood thinks you're such a weirdo."

"Thank you for the compliment," Dr. Jeffcoate frowned. He was busily writing observations in a thick journal. "Now if you would just let me concentrate here for a minute."

Andrew picked up a small motor from a workbench, and began fiddling with it, pulling a lever and spinning a wheel on its side. What is it? he wondered to himself, rolling it over in his hands. Some new kind of roller skate?

"So what do you do down here all day?" he asked the scientist.

Dr. Jeffcoate looked up from his journal. "I give my mind freedom to roam," he said grandly, with a majestic sweep of his hand.

"Had much luck?" Andrew asked, still spinning the motor in his hand.

"Occasionally," Dr. Jeffcoate replied defensively. "For example," he continued, "without that *toy* you're playing with, there wouldn't be a portable dialysis machine."

"Oh!" Andrew cried in surprise. He quickly replaced the motor on the shelf.

"And other times I come up with things like this," Dr. Jeffcoate proclaimed. He proudly held up an aerosol can with the label *Nail in a Can.*

Andrew stared at the can. "Hey, Dr. J., isn't that the super spray glue they took off the market?"

Dr. Jeffcoate shook his head. "Yes. One idiot loses a couple layers of skin, and they make a big fuss. Here. Keep it." He tossed the can across the lab to Andrew. "It's very handy."

Andrew caught the can of spray-on glue and dropped it into the knee pocket of his pants. Then he began to look around the lab some more. "I guess letting your mind roam doesn't pay that much, huh?" he asked.

Dr. Jeffcoate slammed down his writing pen. "Andrew," he said, sounding exasperated, "I'll make you a deal."

"Deal?"

"If you'll be quiet for ten short minutes, I'll do my best to answer all reasonable questions."

Andrew began to catch on. "Oh. I'm bothering you again, aren't I?"

"Yes, you are," Dr. J. replied without hesitating. He went back to his journal and began writing feverishly. "Just give me ten minutes here."

Andrew sat back down in the leather chair. "Right. Not a peep. I promise."

Dr. Jeffcoate smiled from behind his book. He began filling in several long charts.

"Do you think dentists should really be called doctors?" Andrew asked.

"Aha!" Dr. Jeffcoate cried. He pushed the glasses back on his nose and reached for his pocket watch. "Five fifty-two. Your silence lasted for exactly eleven seconds!"

"Five fifty-two?" Andrew's mouth dropped open in horror. "Oh, no! Caroline! I'm late!" he cried. He headed for the lab door. "Gotta run. Catch you later, Doc."

Andrew took off with a blast of super speed. The force of his takeoff practically blew the lab apart. Papers flew everywhere, and Dr. Jeffcoate's hair was nearly blown off his head!

But Andrew didn't notice. All he could think about was how he was supposed to meet Caroline at the Burger Barn at five, and how it was now nearly six, and he had missed their date.

She had given him a chance, and now he had blown it — probably forever.

He ran down Dr. Jeffcoate's long driveway, then screeched to a halt as he saw Caroline walking dejectedly along the sidewalk. She looked up, saw him, then quickly looked away.

"Caroline — wait!" he called to her, feeling as bad as he had ever felt in his life. "You've got to believe me. I didn't ditch you. When I woke up this morning, I was so excited about seeing you, I threw up!"

"Don't try and sweet-talk me," Caroline said.

She started to say something else, but stopped short when a long, black sedan squealed around the corner without slowing down. The car jumped the curb and roared right at the two terrified teenagers.

"Look out!" Andrew managed to scream.

But there was no time to move.

The car screeched to a halt beside Caroline. The front door swung open. Mr. Beech, his steel-gray eyes narrowed in grim determination, leaped out of the car.

He grabbed Caroline in his long, powerful arms.

She tried to scream, but his big hand moved up quickly to cover her mouth.

He pulled her to the black-windowed car, jerked open the back door, and with a powerful heave, tossed her into the backseat.

"Help me! Andrew — help me!" Caroline screamed through the back window.

Mr. Beech leaped back into the front seat. The car began to back up before he had pulled his door closed.

Andrew had to dive out of the way to avoid being hit.

He looked up to see Caroline still screaming to him for help, her hands pressed desperately against the back window of the car.

But he was too stunned, too frozen with fear to move.

The car made a violent U-turn across Dr. Jeffcoate's front lawn, then battered its way through a pile of garbage cans by the sidewalk, sending garbage flying over the lawn and street.

The car just missed a passing truck. It sped

away as Dr. Jeffcoate came running out of his house.

"What on earth!" he cried, first seeing the tire ruts in his lawn, then the garbage strewn everywhere.

He gave Andrew a bewildered look. "Who would — ? It was Mrs. Shellenbach, wasn't it?!"

Andrew still couldn't talk. He stared back at Dr. Jeffcoate and sadly shook his head no.

13

Caroline's father, Jack Niles, paced the living room, his eyes on the black phone beside the couch. "What are they waiting for?" he asked, pounding his fist into his palm. "Why don't they call?"

Andrew and Dr. Jeffcoate sat nervously on the couch, shifting their legs, folding and unfolding their arms, and watching Jack pace.

"I'll kill 'em," Jack declared vehemently. "I'll kill 'em!"

"Emotionally, that would be very satisfying," Dr. Jeffcoate said quietly, trying to be the calm, cool one. "But a more prudent choice might be to call the authorities."

Caroline's father spun around angrily to face Dr. Jeffcoate. His eyes revealed anger — and fear.

"The authorities?" he cried. "They couldn't find

84

a magazine at a newsstand! They're the ones who said no one would ever get near us! They're the ones who told me that no one would find us!"

He slammed his fist hard against the wall. "Two months later — just two months," he said bitterly, "Nate Pelino's goon takes my little girl."

Mr. Niles shook his head. "Some witness protection program," he said sarcastically.

Hearing those words brought Andrew out of his trance. "Really?" he asked Caroline's father. "Who'd you rat on, anyway?"

Mr. Niles gave Andrew a blank look, then resumed his frantic pacing.

"Andrew," Dr. Jeffcoate said in his calm, even voice, "why don't you go into the kitchen and get us something to drink?" And then he added meaningfully, "And take your time."

Glad to have something to do, Andrew pulled himself up off the couch and walked quickly to the kitchen. He felt as if he couldn't have sat on that couch waiting for the phone to ring for another second.

Again and again, he saw the whole terrifying scene from that afternoon in his mind. He saw Caroline standing on the sidewalk, looking so angry and dejected because he had stood her up. Then he saw the black sedan roar into view. He saw the tall man with the strange eyes and the white-blond hair leap out of the car, grab Caroline, and toss her inside.

And most painfully, he saw her pressing against the back window as the car sped away, calling to him, calling desperately to him for help.

While he stood there. Frozen. Frightened.

Useless.

"Call me Captain Useless," he told himself glumly.

"Useless Man to the rescue!"

"Useless Man *not* to the rescue!"

He opened the refrigerator door and looked inside. There were a few cans of beer and a bottle of club soda.

He was about to go back to the living room to ask the two men which they wanted when the phone rang.

The loud ringing startled him. He looked up to see that he was standing right next to the kitchen wall phone.

Andrew heard Caroline's father pick up the phone and answer it in the living room. Then he picked up the kitchen phone, covering the mouthpiece with his hand, and listened in.

"Look — it's me you want," Andrew heard Jack say to whomever was on the other end of the line.

"Let my daughter go. Take me in her place."

There was a long silence at the other end. Mr. Niles repeated his request that they exchange Caroline for him.

Across town in a suite at the Golden Plaza Hotel, Mr. Beech was firmly in control. In fact, things were going just as he had hoped.

The daughter had been easily collected and was being a model prisoner. Bound, blindfolded, and gagged, Caroline had given up struggling to free herself long ago. She sat stiffly in the hard hotel armchair, listening to Mr. Beech, trying to hear what he planned to do with her.

Mr. Beech was pleased that she had stopped struggling so quickly. He didn't want to have to get really violent. He seldom enjoyed real violence. He could do it easily enough. But he always found the threat of violence a lot more interesting than violent acts themselves.

As for her father, Mr. Beech had other instructions.

Her father would get what he deserved.

He was, after all, a rat, a squealer, a stool pigeon.

Niles thought he could get away with it. He thought he could testify at the hearings, then change his name, change his address, change his job, change his looks a little — and no one would ever find him.

That's what he thought.

But he thought wrong.

He didn't give Mr. Beech enough credit. And now it was Mr. Beech's job to show Jack Niles, or whatever he was calling himself now, the error of his ways.

Mr. Niles had to be taught a lesson. Mr. Niles had to become an example to others who might think they could squeal and then get away with it.

Mr. Niles would soon be squealing again, Beech thought with a grim smile. But this time, he would be squealing in pain.

Beech spoke clearly and distinctly into the phone. "Go to the Golden Plaza Hotel," he instructed Caroline's father, his voice businesslike but menacing. "There will be a key waiting for you. Go to the room and await further instructions."

Mr. Beech replaced the receiver. He had a smile on his face. He liked this part. A lot.

In the Niles' kitchen, Andrew silently replaced the receiver on the hook. "The Golden Plaza Hotel," he told himself, repeating the name again and again so he wouldn't forget it.

He squatted down to the cabinet beneath the sink, pulled it open, and began searching inside. It didn't take long to find what he wanted — aerosol cans. There were all sorts of cleaning products under the sink, and many of the them came in aerosol spray cans.

"Ultra Man gets a second chance," Andrew told himself.

Was that excitement he felt in the pit of his stomach? Or was it terror?

He grabbed up as many aerosol cans as he could hold. Then he ran through the front hallway and out the front door.

He leaped into the air, pressing two aerosol cans down to take off.

But something happened. Something went wrong.

He floated up a few feet — and then stopped!

He felt as if something was holding him down.

In fact, something *was* holding him down. It was Dr. Jeffcoate, who had run out of the house after Andrew, and now had a firm hold on Andrew's ankle.

"Andrew — knock off the comic book heroism!"

Dr. Jeffcoate called frantically up to him, trying to pull him down by his ankle.

"Let go!" Andrew cried.

"No," the scientist insisted. "We're talking about organized crime, professional killers. Stay out of it!"

"I can't!" Andrew declared. "I took a sacred oath to defend the innocent and downtrodden. Caroline was snatched from under my nose, and I just stood there and did nothing."

Andrew tugged, trying to free himself. "I'm always saying I'm going to do things, and then I never do," he called down to Dr. Jeffcoate. "Well, not this time!"

With a powerful thrust, Andrew kicked his leg free. Pressing hard on the aerosol cans, he took off, flying toward the Golden Plaza Hotel.

Nothing could stop him now.

He hoped.

14

The town stretched out below him, moving and flickering white and yellow lights against a background of black velvet. That was exactly the way the town had looked the night Andrew had flown home from visiting his grandparents.

Of course, that night was a little different. That night he had been in a plane.

He pressed down on one of the aerosol cans and swooped down low as he approached the hotel. How would he ever find the room where Caroline was being held prisoner?

If only he had super hearing . . . or X-ray eyes.

He'd just have to search every window until he found the right room.

"I'm coming, Caroline," he said aloud, as he lowered himself to look into the top row of windows.

Most of the rooms were dark. In one room,

three people sat around a table playing a board game. It looked kind of interesting.

Andrew swung down to the next row of windows.

"Wow!" Two people were kissing.

"Whoa!" he told himself. No time for that. Remember Caroline is being held by a dangerous mobster. There's no time to waste.

The following two rooms were dark. The next room had an old couple inside watching a game show on TV.

This could take all night, Andrew thought, becoming discouraged. And I don't have all night.

What did they plan to do to Caroline and her father? Did they really plan to kill them both? That was the punishment for being a squealer. But what was the official punishment for being a squealer's daughter?

One floor lower, Andrew floated down to a window where the curtains were open a few inches. He flew close and peered inside.

Yes. This was the room.

There was Caroline. He saw her sitting so still in the tall armchair. She was tied up, blindfolded, and gagged.

"I'll get you away from here, Caroline," Andrew

said, mouthing the words through the window even though he knew she couldn't see him.

He looked around the room. There was a big, mean-faced man with white-blond hair sitting at the table. He was calmly reading the newspaper and eating a big, room-service, club sandwich.

Andrew recognized him at once. He was the man that had leaped out of the black car and kidnapped Caroline. Andrew also remembered how big and powerful the man was.

But he wasn't powerful enough to defeat Andrew's powers.

No way.

Andrew took a deep breath. He floated back a little to give himself running — or flying — room.

He lowered his head and aimed himself at the hotel room window. Then he pressed down hard on the aerosol cans and hurtled himself forward like a speeding locomotive.

His head hit first.

The glass shattered easily.

He didn't feel a thing.

Andrew dived into the room. He came down hard on the carpet. Then he spun around to face the startled mobster.

Placing his hands on his hips and thrusting out

his chest in a practiced superhero move, Andrew announced to Mr. Beech: "Unhand her — or answer to Ultra Man!"

Beech didn't even get up from his chair. He obviously didn't see Andrew as much of a threat. "Beat it, kid," he said, nonchalantly swallowing a big bite of his sandwich.

Then he pulled a large pistol from a holster beside him, aimed it at Andrew's chest, and pulled the trigger.

15

The bullet slammed hard into Andrew's chest.
Then it bounced off and slid down to the carpet. It had been flattened to about the size of a
nickel!

Andrew looked down at where the bullet had
hit him. There was a hole burned into his shirt by
the gunpowder. The hole was right over his heart.

"My new shirt," he said, examining the hole.
"Aw, my mom's going to kill me!"

This got Beech out of his chair. He stared at
the flattened bullet on the floor in disbelief. Then
he turned his look of disbelief onto Andrew.

He rushed at Andrew, his steely eyes filled with
fury. He aimed a powerful punch at Andrew's
face. But Andrew used his super speed to duck
away.

This made Beech even angrier. Again, he sent
a powerful swipe of his huge fist to Andrew's face.

Again, Andrew dodged away, and the blow hit nothing but air.

Beech roared out his displeasure and frustration.

Then he rushed at Andrew again, drew back his fist, and landed a solid punch on Andrew's jaw.

The punch was hard enough to drop any man. But Andrew laughed and shrugged it off. He really hadn't felt a thing.

Beech roared again and his fist slammed into Andrew's jaw once more, this time twice as hard, a staggering blow.

But Andrew didn't stagger.

Instead, he laughed.

In a wild fury, Beech unleashed another powerful punch. This time Andrew ducked. Beech's fist plowed deep into the wall. He howled in pain.

As Beech struggled to pull his hand from the wall, Andrew picked up a wooden chair and smashed it over Beech's back. The chair broke into a dozen pieces.

Beech reeled against the wall, trying to shake off the effects of the blow. Then he came after Andrew, his hands outstretched, breathing heavily, cold fury in his eyes.

"Now, look — you tried to shoot me!" Andrew cried, backing away.

He didn't back away fast enough.

Beech grabbed him by the neck, lifting him off the ground, and started to squeeze. Andrew struggled to free himself, but Beech's grasp was too tight, too powerful. Andrew began gasping for breath.

His hands searched desperately for a weapon, any weapon. As Beech continued his choke hold, Andrew's right hand found something. It was the *Nail in a Can* he had tucked in his knee pocket.

He pulled out the can and pushed the cap off it. "This will stop him," Andrew told himself. "I'll glue him to the floor. They'll have to tear down the hotel to get him free!"

But Beech gave him a hard shake. The can dropped out of Andrew's hand and rolled to the floor.

Beech's hands closed tighter and tighter around Andrew's throat. Everything began to go white, then black.

A loud noise brought Andrew back. What was that crash behind them?

He saw Dr. Jeffcoate burst into the room. The scientist held a baseball bat over his head. "Let the boy go!" Dr. J. yelled.

He swung the bat at Beech. But Beech grabbed it easily out of Dr. Jeffcoate's hands and tossed it aside. Forgetting about Andrew, Beech went after Dr. Jeffcoate. He pinned the frightened scientist against the wall and prepared to finish him off with his fists.

Andrew grabbed the can of *Nail in a Can* off the floor. He ran up behind Beech and sprayed a patch of the fast-acting glue on the back of Beech's suit jacket.

Confused, Beech forgot about slugging Dr. Jeffcoate and spun around to face Andrew.

Andrew sprayed a round blob of glue onto Beech's left cheek. Startled, Beech reached his hand up to his cheek. The hand stuck immediately.

Andrew sprayed Beech's other cheek. Without thinking, Beech reached up to feel what it was. Now both of his hands were stuck to his face.

Andrew shoved Beech back against the wall. The glue on Beech's back held him tight. He struggled to pull away, but Dr. J.'s amazing spray glue was too powerful.

"You little swine!" the furious Beech screamed at Andrew, pulling helplessly in an attempt to free himself or his hands.

Andrew reached up and sprayed Beech's lips together before he could shout anything else.

"Caroline!" Andrew cried. He ran over to her chair and pulled off her blindfold and gag.

"Andrew!" Caroline was definitely shocked to see who her rescuer was!

At that moment, Caroline's father burst into the room, carrying a pistol. "Beech!" he cried, astonished to see the big mobster helplessly pinned to the wall, his hands stuck to his face. Then he ran past Andrew to Caroline and pulled her up into a long, grateful hug.

16

The federal agents came promptly at ten the next morning. Andrew and Caroline stood together on her front porch, watching as four of them loaded the Niles' personal effects into the back of a long, black limousine.

Neither of them knew quite what to say. "How do I thank you — ?" Caroline started, then stopped. It sounded so trite, so phony.

"If I can't write you or call you," Andrew said sadly, "can I at least have a picture?"

"Oh, they're all packed," Caroline said, looking away.

"I'll never have anything to remember you by," Andrew complained.

"Yes, you will." She smiled at him and moved her face up close to his. Just before their lips touched, a voice called, "Caroline!"

The two teenagers broke apart as Mr. Niles

approached. "I — I'm ready, Dad," Caroline quickly, blushing slightly. "I was just saying good-bye to Andrew."

Mr. Niles turned to Andrew. "Yeah. Well, I don't know how you did what you did, " he said, shaking his head, "but I want to thank you for saving my little girl. And you did a nice job on the lawn, too."

He shook Andrew's hand, then hurried back to supervise the agents.

"Caroline, I — " Andrew started.

She interrupted him by pulling his face to hers and giving him a long, tender kiss.

"I'll never forget you," she whispered.

She jumped off the porch and ran to the car. Andrew sadly watched as she climbed in beside her father. She waved to him, a quick wave, a sad, final wave. And then the car pulled away.

Andrew watched until the car was a black speck in the distance. Then he turned to look at the empty house, the empty house that a few minutes before had been Caroline's.

"Come on, Andrew," Dr. Jeffcoate said, putting a hand on Andrew's shoulder. "Come help me with something."

He started leading Andrew toward his house. "Andrew," the scientist said softly, seeing the miserable expression on Andrew's face, "I never read many comic books. But I seem to recall that superheroes seldom get the girl."

"Well," Andrew shrugged, brightening a little, "maybe next time."

Dr. Jeffcoate stopped walking. "Next time? What do you mean *next* time?"

"Sure," Andrew said, starting to regain his old enthusiasm. "We can't stop now. We're a team. Like Flash Gordon and Dr. Zarkoff . . . Captain Kirk and Spock . . . Batman and Robin. . . . "

Dr. J. looked doubtful.

"That *Nail in a Can* gave me an idea," Andrew continued, walking faster, his usual smile returning. "I'll bet you could whip me up a utility belt. You know, like Batman's. Maybe build in some CO_2 cartridges to free up my hands when I fly."

"Now, wait just a minute!" Dr. Jeffcoate said, hurrying to keep up with Andrew. "You almost got us both killed and here you are jabbering on about this comic book nonsense. If I'd only hired a *real* gardener, this never would have happened!"

He grabbed Andrew by both shoulders and made him stop on the edge of the driveway. "Andrew, hold it. Please. You want to run around in a cape? Wait till Halloween. Don't get used to these powers. I'm warning you — I'm going to cure you."

"Cure me?" Andrew looked as if he wanted to laugh at the thought.

"That's right," the scientist insisted. "Until then, I want your word that you won't even think about running around and trying to save the world."

Andrew didn't say anything.

"Come on. Promise me," Dr. Jeffcoate insisted.

"All right, Dr. J.," Andrew said thoughtfully. "I — I promise."

But the grin on his face said otherwise. As did the fact that behind his back, his fingers were tightly crossed.

"White lies don't count at all," he told himself. "Especially if you're the world's one and only ULTRA MAN!"

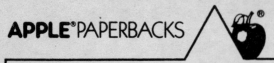

APPLE®PAPERBACKS

More books you'll love, filled with mystery, adventure, friendship, and fun!

NEW APPLE TITLES

☐ 40284-6	**Christina's Ghost**	Betty Ren Wright	$2.50
☐ 41839-4	**A Ghost in the Window**	Betty Ren Wright	$2.50
☐ 41794-0	**Katie and Those Boys**	Martha Tolles	$2.50
☐ 40565-9	**Secret Agents Four**	Donald J. Sobol	$2.50
☐ 40554-3	**Sixth Grade Sleepover**	Eve Bunting	$2.50
☐ 40419-9	**When the Dolls Woke**	Marjorie Filley Stover	$2.50

BEST SELLING APPLE TITLES

☐ 41042-3	**The Dollhouse Murders**	Betty Ren Wright	$2.50
☐ 42319-3	**The Friendship Pact**	Susan Beth Pfeffer	$2.75
☐ 40755-4	**Ghosts Beneath Our Feet**	Betty Ren Wright	$2.50
☐ 40605-1	**Help! I'm a Prisoner in the Library**	Eth Clifford	$2.50
☐ 40724-4	**Katie's Baby-sitting Job**	Martha Tolles	$2.50
☐ 40494-6	**The Little Gymnast**	Sheila Haigh	$2.50
☐ 40283-8	**Me and Katie (the Pest)**	Ann M. Martin	$2.50
☐ 42316-9	**Nothing's Fair in Fifth Grade**	Barthe DeClements	$2.75
☐ 40607-8	**Secrets in the Attic**	Carol Beach York	$2.50
☐ 40180-7	**Sixth Grade Can Really Kill You**	Barthe DeClements	$2.50
☐ 41118-7	**Tough-Luck Karen**	Johanna Hurwitz	$2.50
☐ 42326-6	**Veronica the Show-off**	Nancy K. Robinson	$2.75
☐ 42374-6	**Who's Reading Darci's Diary?**	Martha Tolles	$2.75

Available wherever you buy books...or use the coupon below.

America's Favorite Series

THE BABY-SITTERS CLUB®

by Ann M. Martin

The six girls at Stoneybrook Middle School get into all kinds of adventures...with school, boys, and, of course, baby-sitting!

Collect Them All!

PREFIX CODE 0-590-

Available wherever you buy books...or use the coupon below.